metamorphosis
ungodly transformation

Admer Balingan

Ukiyoto Publishing

All global publishing rights are held by

Ukiyoto Publishing

Published in 2021

Content Copyright © **Admer Balingan**
ISBN 9789364945493

All rights reserved.
No part of this publication may be reproduced, transmitted, or stored in a retrieval system, in any form by any means, electronic, mechanical, photocopying, recording or otherwise, without the prior permission of the publisher.

The moral rights of the author have been asserted.

This is a work of fiction. Names, characters, businesses, places, events, locales, and incidents are either the products of the author's imagination or used in a fictitious manner. Any resemblance to actual persons, living or dead, or actual events is purely coincidental.

This book is sold subject to the condition that it shall not by way of trade or otherwise, be lent, resold, hired out or otherwise circulated, without the publisher's prior consent, in any form of binding or cover other than that in which it is published.

dedication

to all the dead humor,
and sick flowers-
moldy,
bloodshot;
something fragile
something

dear.

acknowledgements

the realization of this collection would not have been possible if not for god, above all, for the gift of words to write.

to a few individuals who have supported and read my works since i started posting them online.

my family, friends, kind strangers, and my fellow writers and poets who have motivated and showered me with magic to make this happen.

especially to Ukiyoto Publishing for this beautiful opportunity and to my lovely raindrops who have been making rhythm with me throughout.

my sincerest gratitude goes to all of you.

the birth

spoiled child

i remember all the days, teary-eyed.
and my skin grows ugly goosebumps.

they are tiny bombs, planted like dead
bodies within a body.

yet, they explode, still-- a slow death,
silent, sneering.

and i remember the squeals afterwards--
like a punished hen,

a criticized spoiled child
without tears.

rose tongue

see this skin-- bruised from
rose tongue and sharp-eyed sun--
i stop calling it Paradise, or a spot on earth
where fairies feast-- a kingdom that glistens
the delight of the moon.

see this skin-- how it grows failed hair,
and worn eyes-- deplorable,

there is no bone, nor tangible magic;
there is nothing here to hold
by hands, ocean-wide--

dazzling blue,
enchanting.

each skin part, an opposite to Jesus'
it is a parable long unspoken in Churches to the flowers--

nothing ever blooms,

metamorphosis

ultraclean,

sweet;

nor all blood shining--

out.

that child

i'll always be that child--
born with a birthmark, bad luck.
like that same old face of
dead magic i remember--

damned, scarred.

since then, i keep aging,
without ceremonies,
or star showers, turning the night into gold.
teeth into rich flowers.
it is the same night,
a body well-covered with bite marks
and fungal
growth.
there is nothing glorifying, to hold with
open hands.

each is a monument
that easily melts in the sun,
each doesn't stand last in the memory of

metamorphosis

the passing years
to remember everything
about
the

child.

birthmark

i let the hours bruise me--and leave me
frail, worn in a corner like a tartar--
retained since birth.
a bad memory of gracelessness,
hung fresh in the old teeth
of the clock, preserving it like
a native sun.

the entire wall is a large face
that carries it, like an unconscious mouth,
fed with dead
Anibong leaves--
it crackles like a
heated oil,
a boiled skin,

well-punished years.

it has a name
i am still learning to
speak,

and make an identity from.

a new birthmark,
i am not used to have

that seems to belong to someone else
with a long dead memory.

and what only remains alive are
empty skulls,
and scattered brains

of the young people
i once closely knew.

each man's grimace

each man in this house is stranger to me.
it's been three years, yet i am still
not familiar with their
faces, names, birthdays, scents;

how shameful!

i am here, at the same time, not.
each day i am becoming more and more

thin, as smokes, dying in the air.
i float as a nameless fish,
one born without a water,

unfelt as a
silent fury, well-managed,

well-kept.

i was born with a poor memory,
a lousy eyes,

metamorphosis

i look at each man like a tangled black webs,

pages full of unwanted,
dirty hand-writings;

no words can paint them, crystallized.
those that are hung, and
remembered by an infant--

i don't know them.

i know only a room, and green moldy windows.
i know only wet mouths,
slippery floor mat
with deteriorated smiles,
and
oiled fishes.

i know only dirty white walls
and orange tarpaulins patching mice holes.
i know only faceless men,
a forgotten birthplace,
and a far-flung house,

quiet.

i rarely talk to them,
i don't think i am allowed to.

the noise is a baby cry when i speak
in a solid, tired evening--

it awakens each man,
and turns each of their snore into a groan,

a
grimace.

childless mouth

it is another day passing like a child,
barefoot and bruised.
one with no name tag,
or address;
it is a skin, an empty document.
it has no pages to flip or burn or eat.
all are but hands that are inkless,

full of grimes.

nothing comes out clear and clean--
immaculate as flowers.
all is as vicious as the sun in the afternoon,
spitting heated saliva on this skin,

that wears no luck.
it is prone to everyday mishap,

and stars don't grant good days or wishes,
they fall as stones and prickles,

salts,
and public noises;

i don't hear one with a gentle throat.
each is spitting sour saliva,
like a mad dog, a hungry dog,

barking endlessly.

there are no unforgettable,
falling
miracles
here
to catch by a mouth.

everything spills in many places,
but not here.

it remains as an empty mouth,
it is a wombless mouth,

i spit no child to call mine.

shallow waters

i feel there is no way to escape from this
ill-luck skin--
a well-confined city. and everywhere is
god's acid saliva,
burning each baby magic.

this skin sweats gasoline--
it incinerates all the child-like hair--
the most tender.

there are no hands as gentle as a comb.
a Mother.
no mouths are sensitive radio,
playing lullabies.

each is razor,
a cruel barber with swollen tattoos and
bad haircut;

always, always, in a bad mood.
miserable,

punished.

this skin
itches
like
hell,
a countless
pests;

and

i don't sleep with well-treated, calm skin.
i don't sleep at all.

i am boiled--
often this body's a cauldron,
fed to the fire.

it spits smokes, flames, bad words;
nothing sounds, feels like Mary-- so immaculate.

flowers have aged,
they become calloused adults

from sunless
rooms--
no life is
well-lived
inside.

it is all as damned as the fish inside of the chest.

i feel it all the time. when i am awake,
and while these eyes,
a sea of ghosts,

ranting.

a fish deprived of lungs.
a fish drowned without mercy.

all are raging,
below the tides,

bottomless,

there is no luck for

shallow

waters.

dead people

people
everywhere have run out of life.
of scent, of flickers.
i feel no emotions, tender in everything
i see and touch--
each is an obese fish, sun-burnt
with red, large
eyes-- formalin soaked,
food for
the
damned animals.

there is no special occasion,
or special to eat, or
something to hold proudly.
each is rotten, each is lousy, each is bland;
no single part is human to touch--
alive.

all are dead humor,
and sick flowers--

moldy,

bloodshot;

it looks less darling--

something fragile,

something dear.

nobody is a skin

each day that arrives doesn't excite me
like an infant.
what glows or comes with
a new hands, still,
doesn't soothe all these defeated parts.
they are the same inflamed parts,
the same damned,
the same wretched,
the same;
and i get bored to see not a
single spark
and more sparks
to touch and
be touched with intense magic-

a
glorious
transformation.

instead,
all there is is another stranded ghost,

a dead floating flower,
and
untouchable
smile
as plain air.

nothing comes with a skin-
well-shaven,
and vivid

as prayers,
as eyes-

so,
so

human.

ode to a cadaver

one lies unknown and distant-
inside this sunless cell-
a pit for junks,
and discarded appetite.

i breathe mostly full rough breaths and
sullen air as fat fart-
i dislike it.
even more loathe it.

men, girls, baby;
what do they know about a soft
boy, slowly rotting into a cadaver?-
soon becoming extinct-
permanently wiped out from the
memory of flowers.

as if powdered coals melted in
a hot air-
soon,
no one will remember

this boy has ever born,

or wailed,

or touched,

or seen.

barks and night windows

this is less divine, or poetic.
this bark that echoes- a song of curse that pesters
the night roses, and blackens its red cheek
with a grime.

this grime is a silent, greedy hands
that rumple bedsheets,
soft sleep.

each second i sink into the ugly noise
i howl a desperate howl that is not heard
as if lungs were already saltwater-filled
that i cannot vomit,
a slow poison,
a vines that dirtily scatter inside,
like feces-
it kills,
it kills.

oh, where are the soft window lights?
or a clean-handed Doctor with lullabies?

i have been sick all day,
i have been having a high, high fever,
dear god, make some miracle explosion!

let the stars soothe the night burns with relief,
tonight, turn the barks into softer songs
and dogs into Mothers.

dear god, i plead for a touch of home,
that swings away bad nights,
sings more, more gentle songs.

so bring all the Mothers to me,
let me rest again like a child in their arms.

taste of cannabis

mosquitoes have spread again
inside this room in which blankets and robes
are no thick wools to hold my
skin, guarded. and repellents are no amulets
that deflect these insects from coming in.
this room, has never been quiet as still
anibong trees and roses at midnight.
there are no soft rests here,
no bird songs and Mother's yellow
branches to swing me, only
hideous lullabies, and
grotesque poems hung on the wind,
everywhere. they swirl around as if dusts from
mad city,
and dirty smokes from
factories, and
i inhale all of them. like cannabis.
i inhale it more often that i fancy mosquitoes
and its bites as Mother's kiss,
touch,
a basketful of love.

a tenderness, i forget it's another
maltreatment.
my stomach has become a
compartment for insects that spoil
the flowers in my blood.
i pump air, only to bruise my breath.
i taste no life. i taste no cherries bloom
on my lips.
only deep sighs, and more deep sighs,
i taste the air hefty as stones.
it's as if drowning the night into the tides.
and tides are stagnant waters beneath my
bed. where each night
eggs are given birth and nurtured on it,
so there will be more mosquitoes growing,
everywhere,

while i have again, to do it more, seeking
more smokes to swallow.

ode to tender years

i have known less what i am doing
here--
barely breathing,
barely human.

what i know--
i am both sick and made of pale flowers
beneath the ash sky--
and the moon is deadened by
a red-sun
it tends to this skin without
moist emotions.

i am--
no-one else but
heat burns,
swollen and cracked,
pestered;
the flies mouthwater
at the
sight

of
me.

i am all the faded features
of twilight,
and morning dews.

this body--
blackened and murdered
by unknown hands.
and no single part of it
flickers gold,
still shines
like a baby's first smile
or flowers in June.

i have been skinned to a nameless body,
split half
into gentle and vicious;
i don't know which am i.

and
what am i doing here, still?

with a tender skin-- gone.
tender age-- rots.

i have been strange--
entirely,
after
the untimely death of bones
of tender years.

the shedding

deity

peel the skin of a deity for me--
let me borrow it,
let me wear it.

it is all delicate, yet, shiny--
one that glistens, like a marble sky.
therefore, magnificent.
therefore, a merriment to the eyes,
to the hands; and
i turn into a gracious one--
all shiny, too--
less damned, less consumed--
and i don't dissolve into air,

i don't go everywhere i am paper light--
intangible.

humans have to stay alive inside here--
occupy me till i am heavy,
till i grow thick skin, too--

unbreakable,
soft like deity's--

i envy, i envy.

i peel every sense-- and i lost appetite,
i lost sense of touch,
i lost sight,
i lost hearing;

as another skin was born,
and another died--

strangers rose,
and walked facelessly.

i become unfamiliar, where i stand.
is this a ground,

or a heaven?

graceless

look upon these graceless hands--
how do i clean them with a prayer?

i have curled them, for so long the bones
hide in shame.

they don't glisten, however i pressed them--
they are stagnant water,

immobile,

waiting as though time creates its own
miracle,
and humans move on their own, and
behead themselves.

this is pure killing--
how do i forgive?

god must have held these hands--
but do they soften?

indefinite

it scares me. for what's ahead, and what's about to happen. i feel completely unequipped, powerless; i don't know what magic these hands have to give me in return.

missing human

then there is this emptiness-- a kind that
blandly whistles to the deaf night,
and wind goes astray with missing hands.
i could touch no one that burns,
and illuminates

even if i pretend i am human.

Sweet Elvie

morning arrives like a body who walks in with a fat news--

wind chimes then fall like watery eyes.

cold floors glisten blue, they prick me--

body and soul.

solemn thunder reverberates--

it sings songs to Sweet Elvie, now one of the

flowers-- odourless.

church bells wail;

how do i quiet them?

inside this chest, mostly-- angels sing of unquiet sorrows,

and poets ache and die on

typewriter keys.

how do i color handicapped metaphors

into moving, animated poems?

it seems the heart is missing the central root.

it seems a human is no longer a body,

an empty house;
it deteriorates, it loses its magic.

losing one dear is not a sweet fleeting occasion--
it kills a part of you forever.

novice

i grow frail– each day i become a limp branch.
each breath– a little movement–
green leaves shiver,
leaves fall like giant fists, knives;

i get sore chest,
sore feet,

sore everywhere.

and i don't get well with bare skin exposed to the sun.
i don't get well with white capsules,
watery palms,
sweet rest;

i know no better Doctor to peel me,
squeeze me,
enchant me;
and bring out renewable, mature human

who swallows sore parts

like air,

and not a novice who trembles,
quivers,

shrieks
like a deteriorated washing machine.

prosthetic humans

mornings spin a dusty, large ancient fan--
very identical to brain-dead dogs that run in circle,
leaving throats,
teeth and furs-- a fake legacy--
they give me red skin,
sore eyes,
lungs enlargement;
that kill flowers,
that maltreat organs-- a defective
humans with prosthetic
heads, lips, arms, legs;
barely moist,
barely raw,
barely warm.

seventh night

it is seventh night i hear again a knock, a footstep;
as loud and fat as elephant's.
the door creaks and opens, like a skin– well-soaked in hot water.

the visitor perhaps,
walks in again, a red-handed Doctor
without a nameplate, faceless–
to peel me off like stems of flowers,
like satin petals;
no longer wearable.

it is seventh night my bed sinks
as wrecked boats,

another session made
over sick body– and cold humans
float dead with popped heads–

eventually a failed
experiment!

the entire room becomes an ocean
cemetery,
it stinks, it stinks, it stinks;

nothing smells, and tastes of alive
sugarcane,
nor there is a body
that emits immaculate albatross.

the Doctor doesn't pray or clean.
perhaps, it has left its hands
in its godmother's womb.

it comes inside without hygiene,
inept visitor,
atop my chest–
then press me hard, press me more
till i am black and spoiled–

till i lose every sense of every tender
magic,
making me perpetually
worse.

dreamscape

perhaps, to escape from these mad insects,
and world eaters– is a pipe dream.
even if a town gets swollen above the roof,
sun-bitten,
a boy's skin; scorched as
bad fishes'.

the roof just becomes a landfill for god-wasted
human whose skin, desacralized.
whose heart, a popped tire.
and flowers grow ill, flowerless, unanimated;
miracles don't grow shiny teeth, face, sense;

and become a shrine,
a boy– white porcelain–
so, so beautiful to touch.

but nothing blooms over hands lacking of
moistness–
no damp streets
kiss a boy, kiss a poet,

kiss a poem;

as if a mouth rhymes to no mouth,
and teeth don't dance and die a cheery death.

i seek for rain, a massive rain till it breaks
the roof,
breaks the boy,
breaks the fish.
till it's roofless– beheaded.

i seek for a boy dying on a
dreamscape.

symptom of human

the night sky is pale blood. it wears the
eyes, as cold as the dead's. the trees are
soft spoken,
but leaves flutter like
extrovert's knife on the marble ground,
dancing like mad
ballerinas.
chanting like perpetual
broken hens.

it is never the kind of night i ask the gods
to visit me on my sick bed.
what sounds around is not as friendly
as Mother's alarm, or as gentle as the cello's.
what comes inside are hands of fake
Doctors, feet of elephants with large mouths–
people come out there, long-necked–
spitting large stones;
they overpopulate my chest, then obturate
all of me;
and build homes out of nails,

i don't know where to touch soft spot
on this body.

i tap my wrist, i tap my neck; for the little pulse
that ignites,
yet it always remains a failed search
for symptom of me,
still human.
of me, still warm.

nocturnal eyes

peel this apple skin-- it is no tender human.
it has its guttered kingdom, and
red Knights sun-bathing with nails,
and folly.
each part darkened like fat bags
under nocturnal eyes.
squeeze it,
till water drains.
squeeze it,
till it's paper-light,
till it dissolves,
till nothing's left to touch.

between two cities

i shut doors away from fat-headed
world– i don't belong there.
my feet have run out of weight,
grown weary interpreting signs,
directions;

now i am feather-light,
just an empty, buoyant skin.

i sit close to the corner, right where
Eyes are never asleep–
my brain on my hands, floating like
senseless balloons–
i pricked them!
and painted black and red– till it blends to
my body perfectly well.

it is as if then a new skin were born,
and new body were formed
and named after not from Flowers, and
well-grown Stomach,

but from series of conflicts between

bones and roots,
inside—

is a wide gap between two cities
filled with dead air,
and bald,
political people;

residing, barely one,
inside this body.
inside this poem.

i don't belong anywhere, permanent—
i belong to one, and no one

both a country,
and not a country.

benediction

this house–
has been a spot for nobody,
people know always an open place,
a cathedral;
with no time restrictions.
Visitors just come in and out
with street dusts, elephant footsteps,
desperate noises, and–
belch smokes!

their mouths crack no music or
lyre softly
played from
heaven.

it is never as ideal as flowers–
such presence, a darling kiss of rain
touched by the gods.

they bring only a skin, featherless–
vinegar-scented– akin to

metamorphosis

the bodies i buried long ago.

it seems they have returned as new
people i so long swear
not to dig, dig, dig;
just leave them untouched

forever like a
departed's heart.

yet, those graves seem too shallow
to believe dead bodies rest there,

in perpetual serenity.

for they grow also a feet, and skin, and faces;
now, completely in tangible forms.
they sound much coming from
a throat,
and become one of the ugly murmurs
that have had hands,
they touch me roughly–

the kind that leave breadcrumbs
for Seraphims to feast on.
till i am all dust, all ash.

till none appear glossy as porcelain
statue of Saint with enchanted
eyes–

speaking to me of
benediction.

kingdom eyes

it is same generation–
a rumpled face– that haunts me.
whose eyes, still a shape of
fake diamonds
that never glisten like boy's
polished teeth,
or girl's freshly oiled hair;

none of the existing forms
can be compared to what
looks godly, young, ripe;

well-refined.

what curse does this back carry?
it's as if a kingdom had crumbled like
a tender age, fruits then become
wrinkled– like a Vendor deep-burnt to the sun–
another face was born, yet still marked
with old generation,

still stuck in a receptacle
where baby heads are dipped and drowned
and baptized into red demons,
still growing thicker skin, larger and
more spacious

yet very glossy,
slippery,

still, don't attract magic,
and wake up kingdoms–

filled with eyes!

heaven's favor

one of the ugliest things i thought i buried long ago is the memory of a skin— both cursed and maltreated— like charred stars. killed good dreams. what i thought, i have moved away with clearer, gentler hands; massively lightweight. but, merciless god, how foolish have i been to think they are gone, when they only shift into different forms, every day; a different hands i unconsciously see as tender as flowers; an Infant's skin good for this skin. how foolish!— to not feel the familiar death from long ago that i have to go through another torment i am misled to recognize too often as heaven's favor.

tender fire

i have a terrible hands for flowers.
each one i touch rumples like an old-man skin--
susceptible to touches--

easily irritated.
i make petals burn--

that is what i do.

i don't pamper them with moistness or
flattery;
to set their mood in utter delight!

i don't lie to grow pretty flowers- but,
i want to grow pretty flowers that last.

and what better way there is
to do it, than
burning
them in a fire

as tender as a
touch?

foreign rain

here–
this very hour, a slow rain–
like a fat drops of stones
and teeth,
corroded by a tartar.

an explosion of stars,
lifelessly falling, festered and
out of shape.

they shimmer ungodly.
and they live in my eyes– now,
a packed horrible place,

degenerated.

it runs out of blood, and gloss
of porcelain,
so delicate.

it is but acid-burnt

looking entirely a crevasse.
a paper skin–
well-drenched,
and torn into cold parts–
like scattered faces!

a thousand of eroded
inscription;

the rain keeps pouring acid,
it brainwashes me

till i am foreign.

the growing

antonym

as i age, my eyes do, too.
i don't think it is a privilege or a curse,
to have eyes,
that mature and peel– like a corroded
skin color,
an erosion of lousy,
chapped lips, overused teeth, tongue,
baby throat;

and they all turn into queer people–
i see all of them in brown, black
gray; with floating heads,
like balloons
festered in the sky.

i see nothing grow and illuminate,
as if the sky– a killed sanctum of
Jack-o'lantern mushrooms,

then are burnt into dust–
large, large, large, and infernal dust!–

as if allergens to the eyes, to the skin,
to the flowers;

nothing looks enormously
appealing,
devotional,
like a shrine, a porcelain church, a grotto;

nothing looks enormously human,
touchable,
like Lotus' stems–
a homage to the hands.
a homage to the eyes.

instead,
everything i see and touch
becomes dwarfs–

boorish ghosts–
these eyes don't light up candles for.

what appear to my eyes–
a completely twisted transfigures–

metamorphosis

viz; the stars become feces,
the suns become as florid as Sexton's hair,
the nights, the streets, the people;
become a black teeth–

walking around–
like a foolish goblin, haunting
for eyes,
for miracles,
for enchantment;

from this body, all-grown– an antonym
of it all.

a troubled march to redemption

a lot of days felt like a fat drums— elephant-weight—
pressed on this body,

as if humans with sharp feet
gambol on my chest, my head;

till my skull becomes a ground—
an absence of clear, luminous flowers.
none ever look well-grown,
well-painted—

well-balanced.
it is everything twisted— as bones,
powdered into a high complex riddles even
the gods look at

with baffled eyes.

what is more horrible than a weight
that grows namelessly?

devouring me in ways,
indecipherable.

i am growing with it like my age–
a troubled transition,

of humor,
and embarrassment as if
a world that dwelt on this back–

as if my name
i take with me like rope cuts,
sun burns, thirsty eyes;

less amiable–
more,
more

god-cursed.

a room full of ears

meanwhile, this human system
starts to look like a sternly blocked roadway.
a tattooed men with corroded teeth standing
like a statue.
before my eyes, a faceless miracle.
an electrified body.
a lifeless lamp post. a city filled
with colorless, malicious people eating rosary.

i am marred completely
by ill-prayers,
and squeezed by their fat fists,
disabling magic to run down,
perpetually.
like a course of blood-- a wild, wild energy.

all seems fleeting like leaves of life,
nothing stays full and wide-awake with delight.

each
drops

dead like a
hair,

sunken eyes, pale lips,
grumbling
as a well-consumed stomach.
all cleaned, well-emptied, lightweight;
from the intrusion of too famished hands and mouths,
nothing has left except deafness--
like a far unreached corner,
uncrowded,

yet full of ears. full of ears.

unlovely scatter

a day is a headless flower, consumed by fat bees.
it is now just a useless body, standing,
well-drained by mouths, as starved as
notary public.

these eyes are paperless-- sunken as old skin,
and words with a color of rust.
of dirty green molds in the gums of a
toothless well.

everything itches like an unwashed skin,
still as sour as sun-dried fishes.
salty-hot,
bruising.

everything loses scent,
sweet scents as peas in the morning,
dewy,
soft, soft, soft.

nothing glistens. a day are stars

not renewed
from unlovely scatter.

like this body,
like this body.

morning ambulance

i've waited for long days for the return of the departed--
a body long gone, away, and untouched.
i am obsessed over its presence,
like a casket starving for flowers, for elegies.

here, is only a vacated rusty warehouse,
cold and
discarded as unused
bones.

there is not a single hand packed with alive people,
or mouth spilling endless conversation, laugh, smiles;
it is all pale silence as over soaked lips and skins.
mildewed, unscathed by a stone-hard magic.

nothing shines a pure gold, as lively as an infant's
eyes.
or sounds of too much
gratification.

metamorphosis

here, is only a wail of stomach leaking with
black fluids.
all unpretty,
all uncrystallized;
a repetitive sight of my unwon upheaval.

here, are my entire damned organs,
deteriorated; and they sound
like another sick morning drizzles rattling
over the roof,

an early,
early

ambulance.

ripe bones

there seems to be no more bones left here
to grind into cinders--
a furious, furious magic.
it's all skin,
and roots,
lousy as these eyes that
lack of blood-- an energy fed into
the deceased mouth
where mushrooms grow feet and crippled--
an entirely ridiculous growth.

it doesn't age, sturdy as the fat trunk.
it doesn't change skin, well-polished. well-shone
as silverwares.
it carries this body like a loose balloons,
weightless,
tarnished,
floating senselessly.

so i rip everything i touch in search of ripe bones.
to take this body. to baptize and bring

metamorphosis

this body to life. to fruition.
i rip even the earth's ovary,
the flowers' genitals,
the baby's stomach;
everything that has life--
i hope so dearly i can find one. a bone
that is as large as the city. as timeless as poems,
and damned poets; a magic.

i rip and swallow everything--
rebelliously.
i've been so hungry, so furious

i learned not
to
be

gentle.

with what is here.
with just
a
skin.

the house rehearsals

it is one of the days the house grows eyes,
and roof is reddened with allergy--
the one that grows with no flower,
no enchantment.
it is a pest from hell with a large
mouth,
ocean-size,
that devours human skin, buildings,
cities;
nameless or known.

it is one of the days the house
is an orphanage
for destitute siblings whose biography
is left in the womb of Anibong--

a Woman--
born with rocks and green glossy hair,

poor and far-flung;

luckless.

the house barely grows a plant,
or a tree.
all are well-shaven yards,

a bland air,
smelling of bad factories.

the house is a public market of sick people
and exhausted vendors,
bald-headed
with well-rehearsed smiles.

and i don't know which is real,
and which is not
and
which smile i need
to
smile
back.

great friends

i never make peace with myself--
i am always at war--
words, stones, nails, flesh;
they wail and snarl like a boar,
a black, thick-haired demon
with hands made of vacuum, and
eyes, a rusty machine,
so irritating.

i breathe a sharp breaths fatter than
a giant's legs
they make the rooftops crumble
into the large
pool of these collarbones.
and melt into countless eyes always glossy,
always shine black.
they see no soft glow as kerosene
to eat.
just midnight lizards stealing
winged termites,
the most lame creatures in my

sight,
a terrible film;

i deplore everything that exists,
moves in front of me--
not a dreamlike story with a
perfect-clean setting,
perfect characters that do not die.

what is so noble about living
without a dream?
a room without clean teeth?
no single magic
to marvel at.
it is all bland to touch,
as dull
air,
intangible body that

my hands grow hands
both sick and resentful,

well-matched,

they make of great friends

with

a

knife.

flowerless head

it is dark--
and cellphone flickers like an
obscene joke,
a salt water
that glides down boiled
marbles on this face;
a
clear
opposite of
Jesus.

deplorable--
and baptized as bad climate,
a body of brittle bones--
that creaks and swears like a strangled
hen at night.

a heartless thunder.

it is no holy face,
or a special greeting card

held with a tender smile--
or pure solicitude.

it is a subsistence--
an offering to the sick god with
large mouth,
ballooned stomach,
as fat as a cow.

it moos and moos out of starvation,
and prayers are too thin to shut it up!
prayers are old, outdated;
a dull, soiled silk, hanging weakly
like a long sluggish neck,
and deteriorated organs--

no
hallelujah
can
beautify.

yellow comb is a thousand teeth of kerosene--
it flames!--

and all the hair are sun-burnt,
all fall and die on dirty white
table with mummified edges--

an altar for
beaten
elbows,

flowerless
head.

morning nightmares

it is in the morning i see most nightmares,
in full form,
hanging on windows-
beheaded
and
skinned
by unwashed curtains.

it is when air is most thick as sack of cements
to breathe in
and out,
heavy as the sour smell
of dirty
laundry-pile,

god-cursed,
and downtrodden.

it is in the morning they have their most
large eyes on the orange walls,
razor-sharp as cat's,

metamorphosis

flaming as sun's-

they vomit boiled heads on this skin-
a fungi,
a bad words
a rusty scissors,
and each,
leaves cuts, salts, fires, gas;

i eat them nevertheless with my
eyes wide open,
pores,
mouth,

i
eat
everything,

i burp flies
and
other
ungodly
animals.

mad grindstone

i think of my skin as a pool- a large mouth whirling
like a mad grindstone.
each object or hand or flower, or fly;
that tries to eat this skin, i eat it whole like my favorite recipe.
golden or bitter, or covered with molds;
it is just the same-
food-
this sick stomach
starves
for.
this pale blood longs to burn with.

and to feel it burn- perhaps
to feel the signs
of a new birth of songs and happy theater plays.
a new skin, a new chest, an Orchestral pit for gentle,
clean-teeth people.
and no more midnight people,
with strangled vocal cords and bad haircuts.

this burn- might be the plot twist of a death play-
so i scratch this skin more often in the quiet,
secret corner where poets drink
and stab their eyes with black pens.

i scratch this skin like it's the most impractical object,
a nonsense humor i tear it down and
watch tiny miracles die more.
i scratch this skin to make a fire flare
like metals to the grindstone,
i want to see it
and hurt my eyes. burn them, too.

i scratch this skin
and even more it feels like dying but not dying.
just pain,
an endless prick here and there,
a leaden sky.
clothes,
skin,
hands,
chest,
eyes;

filled with large water,

but i don't sink,

i float pale,

isolated,

breathless as popped balloons.

daylight curse

what good is this heat of the day to the head?
it only makes of an empty scalp, for sure--
and suffused it with black rashes--
till no more hair
to peel off and eat.

roofs partly crack and sizzle
windows boil and fume red like
a pissed brother's morning face in my room--
it has carbonized the entire ceiling,
and put the wallflowers in a bad mood.

i am very displeased with this ill luck that
i have grown hands, nothing seems to feel gentle.
each one i touch irritates me.
each object that glows in my eyes
sickens me.

what good is this heat of day to the head?--
this sun has a large mouth in which
my large skin fits it well.

but what good is this to this skin
that easily swells ash
as paper in a fire?

what good is this to thin Astilbes
in a room well-compressed with bad words
and sleepless nights?

this ill luck tails around like a sun,
and a fake operatic voice of a Woman--

my neighbor--
and children who sing a broken
chorus
it almost sounds like a shriek
of a breaking throat.
a bruise to the quiet walls.
scratches on wrinkled trees.

a noise as sharp as the sun
and brother's morning face--
a portrait i can hear loudly,

feel,

and smell sour sweats and stinks on

this skin, a white adhesive tapes

eating dust

and ill luck that i groan

with

my

gritted

teeth.

black marbles

i am quiet confused
what this Makahiya flower is
doing in my room.
there is no timid air indoor in the first place,
and well-drained pots, and moist soil,
and better windows
enough to suck the sun in.

it has stem--
glossy as black marbles,
and eyes- thousand of sleepless eyes
instead of thorns.

i thought once it was a modest stem,
yet it flares!
it sneers at me in every blink!--

full of high energy,
undying as young boy's pent-up
desires for flowers.

metamorphosis

and i don't know why i did touch it, too--
even many times i cut,
i did swallow the flower and
it wavered like bad worms salted
in my throat,
itchy as young, rash pubic hair-
full of sin,
full of sin.

my stomach had been a
junkyard for smiles and stems of unsaintly flowers
i swallowed in the past,

both
faceless,
and distorted,

i once thought it'd satisfy
a starved mouth.

this mouth--
well-covered with
wet cobwebs that had never

been dried,

always starving for more,

more,

more.

i ate the Makahiya and the black marbles

became my eyes--

a very deep

pool

of

melancholy that

i killed the walls

and

broke the vases

for

a

laugh.

thirsty eyes

you think you see me
when i peel to you my skin--
my scabs,
my ungodly healing.

have you seen the flesh?
the inside turmoil, well-covered.
the vortex in the bones, and heart
of White Poppies--
soft to the eyes, to the touch--
peaceful you may say, but have you felt it?
the bitter cold and itch of
red sky crying out pale moons--
haunting, engulfing, choking
all the flowers to death.

i doubt you do,
for you have eyes, undoubtedly
seeing wrong signs.

i put on skin, artificial as this smile.

and to you it is my most raw, my most delicate
possession--
what a bore!
what a senseless sight!

i have a large skin, you see?--
both hard and frail as tombstones.

what has been lying beneath here is dead,
and distant corpses,
for a long long time.

still, you hear a happy songs.
and compare my laugh sound to the
baby's- toothless and young,
innocent and less antiquated.

it's hung permanently bright to your ceiling
as ocean of stars, never dissolving
into an ugly groans.
or a melted delight as the years have grown rust-old,
and i started to rot-

i knew too well i'd arrive here.
i knew too well i'd end up here.

skin--

died from

drought,

thirsty, thirsty for eyes.

a body from previous years

i walk with December with our invisible hands,
tangled like vines to the rusty fences.

its eyes, faint moonlight to the naughty boyfriend
that swallows almost ten days of luck for me
to stay wide awake.
flowers wasted, bones are cuffed on bed--
sheets, skin is cobwebbed;
i feel less of myself.

i walk with December as if it was my long-lost
lover or a long-lost half of me, and
i no longer feel like i used to.
all there is, a presence i cannot feel, existing.
there is no candle burning.
no pumping pulses.
no fluttering butterflies.

it is a presence, dead.
it is a presence long forgotten, long buried
beneath the black, fat fir tree.

and there are no ringing bells clinging to it,
nor Santa and Christmas balls, and purple lights
no new stars hanging in the clock
to look forward to.
it still looks as a clock, a bad clock,
a hungry clock from previous years.

i picture nothing but a passing of time.
like how it normally does.
like how human ages and decays year
after a year.

i picture me, as a clock,
as a time that passes, but remains as
buried body from previous years.

stitch marks

i have left so many ugly stitch marks on my face in trying to make it look happy.

pit on my bed

at night, i hear everything most clearly. my heartbeats for instance, that tiptoe into the quiet of the night like a thief that steals the light from my windows. there isn't much softness with them. they are rough stones. they are well-sharpened nails. they are impatient neighbors. they are fishbones and rusty hooks on my throat that bruise the air i heave. my breaths sound much like elephant footsteps, a disaster crashing the walls; and i am terrified each time i hear them. so i often hide my face behind dead hair, and bind my neck with dead marigolds. i do it well each night, digging my own pit on my bed. maybe then they'd harm me no more when they recognize this body, as silent as death.

silent rain

i have crushed my heart and its pieces
become the rain. no One sees it.
One only tells it is cold– a deathlike cold
that rips skin, and pales the flowers–

the heart is overlooked.

it comes from the sky,
and the sky is my chest
where most storms dwell–
heavy and rough as hollow blocks
that are rubbed on me inside,
bruised me red,
and left me nothing but battered breaths.

the sky swallows me, day and night
like a whirlpool with merciless eyes, big
as an ocean that swallows rest,
and the suns in my bones–

i have soon become like the sky that

metamorphosis

when clawed apart,
no honeyed sun comes out.
no yellows, nor blues– no bright colors.

it is completely black as dirty clouds
as if it were the gods' spat curses
but it made no sounds, even of thunders,
or tiny scratches;

it is all, all quiet.

the wind chimes no resentment.
the trees don't grow feet of a saboteur.
the river is a calm blood, yet it burns when touched.

my chest is the sky that rains bits of my
heart that is never heard;
it keeps raining, it keeps raining,
yet it remains voiceless as quiet.

midnights sleep with me

where do i rest this body, scarred
with dirty midnights?

this bed of air seems another place,
not the right place.

it begets bad dreams i have cut and bled
out, these are blood that have turned
into a country, of dogs.

each attempt to sleep,
they race to me, with eyes- so, so
desperate to get back inside my skin.

i feel its noses- a hundred more
noses that brawl to smoke in the dirts clean,
dying to search for doorways;
impatient,
without passion,
no immaculate desire.

it's no safe place in a wrong place.
so i flip this bed of air thrice, and squeeze it
till it deflates, yes,
it slowly faints and dies
before my eyes like a scorched winter.
yet, still, the dogs never shudder into deep
quiet.

i continue to hear them, clearly,
loudly, snarling at my bad deeds.

this, i earn no soft stares,
no tender teeth. i am no immaculate like
any boy god has favored
with good nights, flowerbeds and luck.

i have become a country for dogs.

i am no similar to any boy who lives
free from feces, from dark urine stinks.
and everywhere is calm,
is spotless-
very unlike from where i sleep,

where midnights always sleep with me.

november

what is there to adore in this skin—
that's clamped with candle scents—already
dried, burnt, and flaked off.
here, are only flowers looming
like a twisted twilight in Poe's eyes—
a grotesque reflection of his deranged
daydreams, of his self-made vultures, pecking
at his own skull.
this skin— covered with spoilt burial moss
and cracked epitaphs— in which
prayers are no tonic, no divine rains
that soothe
that kiss
that caress
that redeem
this skin from the mouth of death.
yet i am a little fascinated how it meanders
on, and all over my skin like a sweats adored
by black flies with ebony eyes
at scorching midnights—
i am fascinated,

that i adore to feel more of
the flies, too. to hover on me, feast on me.
i adore the bruises they engraved
as if my name on a crucifix.
where the priest,
the flowers,
the mourners recite it, and cry over it
with a false
lament that dampens their eyes.
they never rhyme to the whimpers
of a mother's loss.
my name is held as candles in their
hands and thrown into
an open casket instead of soft daisies
to burn, and burn,
and burn more
this skin already dead,
until i turn into a candle scents
only remembered in november.

hear the birds pecking at your windows

it's become one of my rituals to
summon all the birds at night
before i prick my eyes to sleep.
i chant poems to them instead of writing
'cause it feels sometimes pages
have no ears to hear me.
pages have no voice to
echo to you what's itching inside this throat,
every night, inflamed by
i love yous that never sound the
same when mixed with metaphors.
when making love to the inks of these hands
seems wrongful that when i put them
all down on pages, they still look unwritten.
this, i say, your name,
has no longer a place on these pages.
your name belongs in my mouth now–
a rhythm i compel the birds to not forget.
to carry on their beaks.

and i wish, sometimes, the birds carry my voice to you

by pecking at your windows--
loud, successive, almost ragin--
until your windows leak, and
get broken. until the glasses rattle to the
foot of your bed, to your bedsheets, to your
blanket, to your eyes.

i wish, sometimes, you won't hate the
birds for waking you up.

barber's razor

my hair was growing fast when
it was only cut yesterday.
the barber must have tricked me.
the barber's sweat must have crawled
as lices that bore spells of a
voodoo– black as charred moths that
made love to the sound of his
razor, temporarily giving me elation
from every weightful of frizzy red hair
and chipped off worms from the
sun's decayed skin.
i fell believing i had cut my hair clean
from all the ugly moans of
late night whales inside my head.
that my hair already stopped sucking
the viciousness of its waves to
the bonfires in the hands of the
barber. that my hair was burnt softly,
cut beautifully short.
but i might have only fallen into his
bewitching eyes that glinted of

sweet mischievous moon spells to believe
this was not some kind of torment.
i might be only enchanted by the
tongue of his razor that licked my
hair that didn't mean to cleanse me
but only to grow more of fat worms
that curled down and itched on my
face like bad dreams
i ate last night.
i fell believing it was escape
to cut my hair short for awhile
by his hands,
by his razor.
that there was a promised solace after,
at night, or any hour,
but that barber was a pure liar.
'cause there were no hairs that were cut short.
and they were only kept
and buried in his hands, but they
were never dead.
they were still as alive as vines,
still
sticking

everywhere.

sundays devoid of flowers

i was buried deep in this ground
where flowers never bloomed
yellows. where stones
and dusts were sharp
mouths that cut skins,
leaving no apologies
on my medicine chest
that i could reach out to
to mend all the bruises
on my sunday mornings.
i had stitch marks of the suns
all over but
that didn't quite the slow
whimpers, or soothe
ill bodies,
this body
with empty bones
and crippled shoulders to lift
the immensity of the grounds
and crash it in front of the
sun–

bold,

unsorry,

rebellious

to dry off all the ugly morning

dews clinging

like bad omens on the

pastures.

on the balusters.

on my windows.

on my chest.

i was buried 6 feet underground,

and my veins were roots

sprouting

as flowers

that waited for sundays

that never,

never

came.

blackbirds in my eyes

i talk to the wild plants growing
everywhere at my yards like feces
of black-eyed birds,
almost everywhere. and its scent
clinging firmly to the air, as
dirty, rancid flowers
sewn to the fabrics enwrapping my mornings.
i wake up to this, with unchanged
clothes, heavy from cursed
nights that sigh of torrents
on my bed. i am all unwashed
body. and face. and hands,
walking outside devoid of miracles.
and there are plants with open mouths
everywhere that i pluck close
for a redemption.
a conversation. deep,
deep conversation,
nonstop.
my lips have held bagful
of dimming sunsets

metamorphosis

i talk about each of them to the plants,
yet what i heard in return is only a lash,
beheading themselves,
one by one.
and each,
pecked by black
birds, hungry as my eyes.

perpetual fever

how long have i been away?–
weeks or months– of drought, as colorless
eyes. entirely absent,
and poverty-stricken.

there are no large eyes, black and white,
erupting rich flowers. of energy, flaming
like aggressive cars.

they are as slow, and lousy as
unfortunate intellectual,
whose feet, a stone and blood, a stone,
words, a stone;
they don't age or ripen
into a miraculous erosion!

they are stagnant fever, a perpetual itch of an
unwashed molds;
they stick around like a bad dream.

and each hour of being

conscious, or awake becomes
a shortfall. an absence. an aching
teeth, gums; bleeding stale odor,
without words that console, like a pat.

i forgot i've ever had the words
to speak or write without being
beheaded.

most of the days i don't recognize them,
most of the days i recognize
only their heads.

and their bodies seem untouchable.
long buried,
somewhere far and deep; unknown.

most of the days,
i recognize only a deserted breathing,
a stomach, just

a tankful of air.

destitute proprietress

i don't know what is inside of this chest.
it has been quiet here, pale and thin.
i don't know where all the good, fat humans go.
which skin they move into.
which room they wake up in, every day.
it is now a vacant rent house,
far flung,
with sleepless windows
and destitute proprietress.
there is no one here to call,
feel,
it is a white space,
dull, deaf, cemented;
full of hung sick flowers,
discarded clothes and cold skin.

most of the time i wear them
like a teeth and smiles
owned by nobody.

most of the time i am nobody,

exactly like the departed ones,
featureless,
a complex portrait
to
decipher-
a black riddle stuck between the
faded lines,

a tangled ligatures to no
wounds,

chest's
cut
more
open,

exposing fat air,
lifeless

humans.

the transformation

rarity

i spent the entire afternoon wandering. it was a brief experience, yet filled with magnificence. my feet met its rhythm and i– met am. i got to touch my disconnected parts, and give them names after long years of being unknown. how beautiful this reconnection i was favored of. albeit momentary, i knew so well i lived that part so beautifully rare.

faceless wind

i collect every fallen hair,
and put them back on spaces
on my head.

there must be no dead-white space–
it must not become foreign–
like a faceless wind. it must not rust,
it must not turn into one i can't recognize.

it must stay there– like that alive part–
and i have lost none.

i should be complete.
i should be whole.

i should be that.

stationary

it is what i call magic. a moment so slow, so gentle; you can touch the moving without going on a race. you can capture perfect angles without distorting your eyes, constantly switching, adjusting them to different directions. it is magic when it moves you even on your stationary moment. just sitting with a quiet heart, while listening in awe to the magnificence of the world far from the crowded places– just you and the birds, just you and the grasses, just you and the tender wind– it is on these kinds of days or moments i am mostly touched. enchanted.

a slow down note

take a moment,
a slow moment to sit with time.
look intently, into its eyes, and
write a word, for example 'depthless'–
you don't need much, other words to sound
immersive.
write what you see, even just the plain
surface,
even with the absence of rhyme. of melody.
let the words come out, in their most naked.
in the most unprepared occasions.
the thing is that,
they will still look inviting,
even in their most unlovely state,
they will still smell of sweet peas. of you.

you can't be read less by being
less intricate.
you don't need much words
to write.

jesus wears skirt

i have walked in and out of this room,
a bald pit of hell,
like it's meant to stay that way.
but i don't flicker like cats in the red oven,
exuding black smokes,
and burnt hairs.
i don't stink, i smell of Jesus
in a long modern skirt,
filled with *banality*.
like how a boy is called wearing
a light brown skin similar to a girl's,
smile similar to a city's,
sound similar to a sewing machine's
poems similar to the dead's;
all
seen outworn,
all bruised with
prickles–

a community of mouths
of the Cross,

artificial as a wooden
tongue,
that speaks to no Christ.
that speaks only to themselves.

this room is a gentle place.
this room is a kingdom.
this room is heaven.
this room is angelic.
this room is godly.

it is no burning pit,
or bad station
for a girl
or boy,
or *banal*
who wants to
drop
by.

summer miracles

to see the blue sky circling above
your head,
i see clear miracles,
a rebirth after the storms.

and the smoke flight of plane on your sky's body
is a cat's cotton
furs, soft enough to not bruise you, or
leave you scarred all night,
even in your deepest dreams.

summer leaves born and die and fall on your skin
like a morning dew, a slow rainfall;
cold yet never send
you ugly shivers.

it is not often as bad as what you think about the cold,
or rain, and on days you only recognize
storms instead of yourself,

you actually recognize miracles
and the beauty of it all.

home in the scent of anibong trees

here is where my root is buried,
on this sun-baked land that
is seen through the bruises on
my father's hands-
calloused, almost numb, wrinkled
as drought- but it held more than
just dirts athirst for morning dews
and serious cleanses.
they are folktales in the dirts,
both golden and green- a richness
only a rich heart can see.
here is where I first became familiar
with home in the scent of anibong
trees perfumed on my brown skin
like a memory I scratch my way back
to, everytime, and I feel no sting nor skin burns,
only a native mother's softness,
only words rarely spoken,
but felt everywhere.
they are inside me, like
a toothless child, a stubborn teenager,

a curious adult; all browned skin,
all sun-baked,
yet soft, yet soft

flowers not guns

flowers, not guns
i see bullets not as a consolation to angry Father–
it soothes no heart,
smoothens no cathedral walls,
cleanses no dirts.

skin is no ground for bullets
skin is for touches, soft breeze,
caresses, flowers.

it is no burial pit for a Mother's body.
or son's, or daughter's.

flowers, not guns.

guns are for cemented hands,
a soulless bones, a sun without yellow.
they are for hardened chest,
cold and pale as death of marigolds
in the hands of a god.

i call for saints to bury bullets and turn them
into prayers. grow into flowers before the
feet of a saboteur.

i call for the grasses to linger
around like half nightmares and half miracles
that haunt,
that haunt
the god with a fake badge.

let prayers turn into black miracles,
an earthquake
that make the god crumble from his metal
chair.
let his knees clutter like crushed bullets
as if a vomited charcoal from the night sky.

and let his wind, street, river, ground, be charcoaled.

besides,
miracles don't fall clean over dirty hands.
miracles are not for god with a fake badge.

and only when god has become one of the charcoals,
only from there
the flowers can grow more in
the orphaned eyes.

the bell sound

these knees often crumble at the sound of the
church bells. my heart quickens after,
elephants stomp on my chest.

i swear the sky is callous!

i am no pissed-tongue, yet the sky is
too, too thick with dirty nimbus,
and numb stars as cemented bones.
so what magic there is
to clench my tongue in soft quiet?

i feel no course of magic to remain calm.
inside i am pested like a rotten farm yards,
itching all over.
i fume with red air, and
the moon knows it is no magic.

i am no magic.

to see church in clearest bird's view

that is growing bigger, fatter as the sky;
in which the gods have probably
ransacked more handful hands,
and chewed the hands after,
and burped them like a bell sound
that echoes, displeasingly–

i am no fond of magic. particularly this,

that i peck at every bell, disgusted.
i peck at the church's windows,
spitting stones inside.

there is no magic to slow these eyes
that have seen the sky, in its bareness–
most gray, most hideous.
that i feel its every rain as no
nurses to these wilted marigolds,
to this skin scorched by a bell sound–
another flower died.
another fallen dusts to not
blind, and bruise my eyes.

twilight

the sky has been icy these days that
make rooftops shiver by the heavy
blow of the wind.
and cold flower heads, dulled leaves flutter on
my room windows, tapping like wounded
butterfly wings who seek for sleep-ins,
chimney fires and tender
hands. 'cause gardens outside have
been replaced with a warehouse for corpses.
and a once green foliage now rots, now a
dirty site, embedded with unkissed limbs,
decayed twigs, stale flower stems and
petals, infertile soil.

there have been no trademarks of the sun rising.
no sun that is ever drunk with yellow rains.
it's all been as black as fogs
from a contaminated womb of the earth.
in which colors have just become an illusion.
softened air is a ghost to skin,
scarcely felt. only cold– bruising the skin,

mowing skin hairs, till i am all bare,
peeled off, exposing ill-treated midnights
beneath.

i loathe the butterflies, the windows,
the weather for dimming the embers
in these irides and make
eye pits hefty with black tears.
i cry an ugly cry that the cats on my roof
howl and scratch for sunshowers
to thaw the frozen melancholy around and
inside this place.
so i scratch more this chest, too, scratch
more to break it.

perhaps then,
the butterflies will stop coming,
tapping on my windows when this chest
is already empty, all-consumed by
my nails.

nights, perhaps then, will be quiet and calm.
and outside will be as soft as twilight

that rooftops grow flowers for,
and earth
grows more garden,

emits more tidy, finally lighter air.

a habit

i make it a habit to write what i am so powerless to say. there is more than just magic in written words. i feel courageous when i write.

will nights ever get kinder?

i pray, my nails would tear away the thick night skins that carry bad fluids and acid poems until i bare myself clean. until my body's loosened from paperweight– free from hefty vandals, and odors of inks from ill poets' bones. i pray, my nails would grow mouths against my own skin with a desperate urge to devour it. devour everything it keeps. devour all the ugly scratches, and midnight bites, burns, infection– devour, devour, devour, until i'd turn to completely nothing. until it's only air left to swallow.

folktales

evenings are slow flames underneath my bed sheets. and each hour that passes— they age, they grow, they become mature, and as drunk as mouth of the sun that vomits ugly burns on my back. this is a body infection i want to slip away from this bed. each night my hands, and my legs— everything aches to wander somewhere far without bearing the scent of burns and skin fevers. yet here, perhaps has been marked to be my only place. here, is where i am supposed to surrender all my nights to. there are open doors, open windows, open curtains— but what right do i have to get up and touch them? when my hands, and my legs are no longer named after me, but they are already my bed's. i am here only to be burnt and ground into cigarette dusts. with no monuments for my skeletons— and no beautiful folktales for my name.

i stroll outside as a shaven tree

for once, to be outside never feels like a prison.
the stones are no shackles.
the grasses are no vicious makahiya,
pricking the soles of my feet to its fatal impairment.
for once, i walk barefooted without shuddering to tread
on wet cold hallways
where the dogs' bones bark at
the noise of my footsteps,
and my shadow bears no prayers to subdue
them,
to twitch their throats into soft moans.

for once, i walk serenely. as a tree shaven
from all the bones,
leaves,
flowers,
fruits
that are born in all the midnights my mind
is devoid of calm.

daydreams on my desk

for awhile, poetry is an old friend, taking me to the depths of the earth, to unknown pits when silence soaks the moon on my desk— and take me far, far, from the surface, away from my friends here that bear sharp-edged razors of midnights on their flowers that i am so afraid to touch. i wish i didn't touch. and now my hands are lacerations that ache down on my shadows. all over my bones. but for a while, poetry is wandering. patching, unremembering hideous wound marks on these hands. for a while. for a while. i'm breathing clean, and anibong is home tiptoeing on my hair, on my skin, softly. lovingly. for a while, i sink into this sweet fleeting reverie that blurs all the bitter recollection of mornings. for a while, and tomorrow i have to resurface. tomorrow and meet the flowers again. and touch them.

burns and bruises

still, i get trembled at the thought of a night.
lips start to become dead white to feel it through
misty air,
cold flowers,
lacking of so, so much warm rose blood that
they shut like a coffin
on a final burial day.

each tooth is corroded with silent pleas.
each has stopped making a popping sounds
loud enough to compel the time, and
cease it and tie it to the sun.

i communicate through my silence alone.
i have been doing it pretty well,
for twenty years, yet still i fail miserably hard--
still, i often get mistaken.

the night has blurred my identity,
most of my parts are sent into its complete blackness-
to where no words are heard,

no movements are seen,

no colors flickering through like stardusts--

a pure, pure dusts.

everything in the night is folded with deception,

in which my silence is often heard as and mistaken for soft rest,

a calm skin and bones--

peaceful, peaceful moonlit flowers.

when silence is that every horrible,

haunting,

that the night often lies about to be beautiful,

and

i'd like more to stay under the sun, and be skin-tied with it,

all bare and honest,

regardless of the burns.

regardless of the bruises.

sunlit daisies

speak to me in silence, i will listen to you forever.
words, as you know, are mouths--
both populated and festered--
each rarely emits bare
flowers, a scent as pure as

organic skin.

speak to me less,
but more tender, like Infant's eyes,
both innocent and human;
without public noises, or
sudden rise of hard tones,
and bad traffic;

nonsensical.

speak to me with your eyes--
let me see sunlit daisies all over your
bones, as well as
the crushed stars,

the beating heart.

speak to me with your hands, your body;
all your senses that don't make up with words.
speak to me with bones instead--
with life,

tangible magic,

madly,

tenderly felt.

impossible heavens

i bury my hands in my mouth
to search for depth inside my chest.
perhaps, there lies
a well of stranded magic,
or dead Irises, just waiting to be
touched,
and stirred,

till revived.

perhaps then,
this body will finally grow grass,
green– energetic, wide-awake,
radiating–
as mesmerized eyes,
a color,
so delightfully human
which looks free of hands,

vicious hands;
till i stand without a memory,

metamorphosis

of skin, body–
haunted by leaves and
blades.

till i stand,
highly favored with more new skin,
gentler body,
making them more, more

touchable,
less desperate,
less vicious,

less unkind.

i bury my hands in my mouth
in a wish i could hold both solid
and tangible magic;

so, perhaps, from there i will shimmer.
from there i will borne more flowers,
and forget

i ever stand upon one of the grounds,
made up from
a thought, or a tale
about impossible heavens.

a lone flower's point of view

is it wrong to sit on a cold chair outside
while the sky's menacing— sleepless,

as hefty as eyes— red and worn?

waiting,
waiting,

for the streak of something luminous,
of something white that falls,
of something with hands and feet
like a lover's
that dally from the sky
to the chair, to the heart;

is it wrong to soak in the cold—
red lips crack, tongue hanging out, teeth
corroded? petals— no longer shine.
a body— flowerless.

waiting,

waiting,

for little magic that soothes the night,
for little magic that quiets the lone flower.

waiting,
waiting,

for a sun-dappled human
everywhere–

to the green pastures,
to the gigantic trees;

till the night becomes a day, till the cold
turns into a warmth,
a love to a touch,
a night will be quiet;

but it will be the kind that sings.

church songs and bullets

perhaps i was just hands dipped into the angry waters in front of the church. and that i was meant to be skin-bruised and swollen with ugly prayers of the priests, worshippers, and gods that tasted of sea salts in my mouth. they were never soft. they were sheer microbes with vicious fingernails that slowly ate the flowers in my lungs. this was why i breathed out, only air that contaminated mornings that never gave birth to the stars that was named after me. the birds plummeted like bullets on my roof– and they never sounded like softer rains, nor felt like soft suns to my skin– instead i became a landmark for bullets, and beneath was my cemetery. i was skin badly, badly treated and there seemed to be no more church songs that could ever soothe them. there was nothing on here that sang my name with tender mouths. only bullets, only bullets. and my hands that were supposed to shelter me were angrily chewed by the church. my hands, then all of me. but i'd never dissolve into silence. the bullets in my body would still make noise after my death.

metamorphosis

don't search for an old skin here,
that as tender as a child- it
no longer belongs to me.
you can find nothing except blisters,
a failed attempt to refinement.
a leftover of ungodly metamorphosis.
i left it somewhere else- far and unspecified.
i left it in a small-room without an address.
i left it on a faded road signs
leading to no direction.
i left it beneath the disarray of drunk trees,
full of bad luck twigs,
flowerless;
where nothing else falls
except bones,
black hairs,
and worn out smiles.
no longer in use.

i am delighted of the new-found skin,
and to not feel the same way.

but i am not enthralled like by a miracle,
or as if a finality had occurred
to not ask for more.

i have parts that easily rust, always
changing while
others need to be discarded in time.
i don't want them stay long
like a scars,
a blisters

i want another, more,
unending.

About the Author

Admer Balingan is a 20-year old Filipino poet and writer. He is currently a 4th-year teacher education student. He has published poems under Spillwords Press while some of his written pieces were included in local book anthologies. He continues to express himself through sharing his poetry and essays in his Facebook literary page.

He is an aspiring poet, writer, essayist and teacher who often writes unconventional types of written literature. He finds enchantment wandering in the dark corners where lights are quiet ceilings and timid wallflowers, and floors are as soft-spoken as introverted neighbors. He adores the rain, the sky, the wind, the flowers and the water that flows in an uncommon and abstract direction. There he finds beauty– in a most perfectly complex sense. To him, that is where poetry comes to life, and that is where he was born.

www.ingramcontent.com/pod-product-compliance
Lightning Source LLC
LaVergne TN
LVHW041842070526
838199LV00045BA/1394